Be Truthful

Dear Parent:

In childhood, itchy rashes are almost as common as a sore throat or runny nose. Bug bites, poison sumac, poison ivy, eczema, peeling sunburns, medication allergies, as well as the rashes whose causes we never know, are just a few that come to mind. So virtually every child has heard some adult say, "Now, don't scratch." But even after nodding in genuine agreement to the idea of "hands off," most still succumb to the overwhelming urge.

Adults, incidentally, don't have much better resolve. But can we say we've been dishonest, or are we all merely being human in the face of something as compelling as an itch? Temporary relief is so sweet that we can't resist it—even in our sleep. Then, a visit to the doctor (the vet, in Clifford's case) is the obvious next step. But almost as compelling as scratching a big itch is the temptation to avoid taking that trip. Is it only children who say something like, "Oh, my tummy ache is all gone," or, "See, I'm not coughing anymore (*cough, cough*)," when we hear the words, "Go see the doctor"? Some adults also drag themselves around, insisting all the while that they feel fine, or "It'll go away in a few days."

Being truthful is a great goal, but denial has a power of its own when we sense that the truth could lead to something most unpleasant. At times like that, children (and many adults, too) need to borrow the strength of a wise and loving person. Fortunately for him, Clifford has Emily Elizabeth. And your child, happily, has you.

Adele M. Brodkin, Ph.D.

Visit Clifford at scholastic.com/clifford

ISBN 0-439-22006-8

Library of Congress Cataloging-in-Publication Data is available

10 9 8 7 6 5 4 3 2 1          01 02 03 04 05 06

Printed in the U.S.A.   24
First printing, May 2001

# Clifford THE BIG RED DOG®

# An Itchy Day

Adapted by **Peggy Kahn**

Illustrated by **Jim Durk**

**Based on the Scholastic book series
"Clifford The Big Red Dog"
by Norman Bridwell**

From the television script
"An Itchy Patch" by Anne-Marie Perrotta and Tean Schultz

**Cartwheel**
·B·O·O·K·S· ®

SCHOLASTIC INC.

New York   Toronto   London   Auckland   Sydney   Mexico City
New Delhi   Hong Kong

I'd like you to meet my dog, Clifford,
In case you have never met.
Clifford's the sort of a creature
That most people never forget.

As you see, Clifford's perfectly happy.

His red tail is wagging away.

But he was a dog in a dither,

And that was just yesterday.

Have you ever had poison ivy?

Have mosquitoes buzzed right through your skin?

Then you know how it feels to be itchy

And what you do when those itches begin.

And maybe your mom says,

"Don't scratch, dear."

And maybe your dad says it, too.

But, oh, when an itch gets to itching,

**scratch!** is what you want to do.

Something had given poor Clifford
A troublesome itchy patch.
Like you
        and like me
                and like anyone else...
Clifford
        started
                to scratch.

Whatever Clifford has or does
Is never, *ever* small.
Clifford scratched his patch
On a tree.
The apples

began

to fall!

Some bounced off the librarian

And Samuel, who was passing by.

They saw what Clifford was doing.

They guessed the reason why.

Clifford *had* to scratch that patch.

His itch would not be quiet.

Clifford saw a traffic light.

His itch said, "Try it! Try it!"

While Clifford rubbed his itchy spot,
Traffic was tied up in a knot.

If you have a dog, cat, or gerbil,
And that pet is acting upset,
You'll want an expert opinion.
You'll get that pet to a vet.

My dad said, "If Clifford keeps scratching,

We'll have the vet check him out.

Maybe he has an infection...

Or it's nothing to worry about."

Now, who knows exactly what
Dogs think or what they discuss?
Do Clifford and his dog friends
Talk together just like . . . us?

What's a vet?
Do you know?
I think that I might
Have to go.

Perhaps that made Clifford pretend

His itch was at last at an end.

He tried to hide his problem from me

By rolling and rubbing when I couldn't see.

But the itching was driving him

　　Out of his skin.

And he rolled

　　And he rubbed

　　And he tried to scratch

That simply **unbearable** itchy patch.

He ran down the beach and saw the dock.

He started to scratch!

It started to rock!

The boats began to bob and bounce

As if they didn't weigh an ounce.

But Clifford was in paradise.
To scratch, scratch, scratch
Felt oh, so... nice!

The waves began to roll and rise.

The tide grew high before our eyes.

Luckily, my dad and I

Were there to stop the big red guy.

Come on, Clifford.

I bet you know

Whom we need to see . . .

Where we need to go.

Clifford's patch might be itchy yet,

But now he's fine, thanks to the vet.

The vet mixed cream and it felt nice.

Sometimes good friends give bad advice.

Clifford was scared,

But in the end

He learned that the vet

Is a dog's good friend!

So remember, if you're not feeling well,
A grown-up you trust is who to tell.
Don't say, "I'm fine," if you are sick.
Don't try to play a Clifford trick.

# BOOKS IN THIS SERIES:

*Welcome to Birdwell Island:* Everyone on Birdwell Island thinks that Clifford is just too big! But when there's an emergency, Clifford The Big Red Dog teaches everyone to have respect—even for those who are different.

*A Puppy to Love:* Emily Elizabeth's birthday wish comes true: She gets a puppy to love! And with her love and kindness, Clifford The Small Red Puppy becomes Clifford The Big Red Dog!

*The Big Sleep Over:* Clifford has to spend his first night without Emily Elizabeth. When he has trouble falling asleep, his Birdwell Island friends work together to make sure that he—and everyone else—gets a good night's sleep.

*No Dogs Allowed:* No dogs in Birdwell Island Park? That's what Mr. Bleakman says—before he realizes that sharing the park with dogs is much more fun.

*An Itchy Day:* Clifford has an itchy patch! He's afraid to go to the vet, so he tries to hide his scratching from Emily Elizabeth. But Clifford soon realizes that it's better to be truthful and trust the person he loves most—Emily Elizabeth.

*The Doggy Detectives:* Oh, no! Emily Elizabeth is accused of stealing Jetta's gold medal—and then her shiny mirror! But her dear Clifford never doubts her innocence and, with his fellow doggy detectives, finds the real thief.

*Follow the Leader:* While playing follow-the-leader with Clifford and T-Bone, Cleo learns that playing fair is the best way to play!

*The Big Red Mess:* Clifford tries to stay clean for the Dog of the Year contest, but he ends up becoming a big red mess! However, when Clifford helps the judge reach the shore safely, he finds that he doesn't need to stay clean to be the Dog of the Year.

*The Big Surprise:* Poor Clifford. It's his birthday, but none of his friends will play with him. Maybe it's because they're all busy. . . planning his surprise party!

*The Wild Ice Cream Machine:* Charley and Emily Elizabeth decide to work the ice cream machine themselves. Things go smoothly. . . until the lever gets stuck and they find themselves knee-deep in ice cream!

*Dogs and Cats:* Can dogs and cats be friends? Clifford, T-Bone, and Cleo don't think so. But they have a change of heart after they help two lost kittens find their mother.

*The Magic Ball:* Emily Elizabeth trusts Clifford to deliver a package to the post office, but he opens it and breaks the gift inside. Clifford tries to hide his blunder, but Emily Elizabeth appreciates honesty and understands that accidents happen.